DOODLE CAT IS BORED

Kat Patrick & Lauren Farrell

SCRIBBLE

18–20 Edward Street, Brunswick, Victoria 3056, Australia
2 John Street, Clerkenwell, London, WC1N 2ES, United Kingdom
3754 Pleasant Ave, Suite 100, Minneapolis, Minnesota 55409 USA

First published by Scribble in 2017
This edition published in 2020

Text © Kat Patrick 2017
Illustrations © Lauren Farrell 2017

Printed and bound in China by 1010

9781925321883 (Australian hardback)
9781911344131 (UK hardback)
9781950354344 (North American hardback)

scribblekidsbooks.com

I am Doodle Cat.

AND I AM BORED.

EXCUSE ME EVERYONE I AM BORED!

HALLO?

Does anyone even care?

ANYONE?

What's this for?

Can I eat soup with it?

Can I dig with it?

Can I dance with it?

I can doodle whatever I like.

Here's a fancy scribble.

Here I am broken into pieces.

Here I am back together again.

Here I am surfing through time and space

on a wave of farts with Wizard Susan.

Here's six pangolins.

It's a pangolin party!

Here's my bum.

Here's some delicious spaghetti.

WAIT, NO, DON'T EAT IT!
It's Uncle Noodle Cat!

Sorry, Uncle Noodle Cat!

I am Doodle Cat.

And I'm not bored anymore.

What will you draw?